She turned; I saw her turning

MUSHTAQ AHMAD
&
NABI NAZEER

MAHAVEER PUBLISHERS
New Delhi

Published by
MAHAVEER PUBLISHERS
4764/2A, 23-Ansari Road
Daryaganj, New Delhi - 110002
Ph. : 011 – 66629669–79–89 Fax : 41563419
e-mail : mahaveerpublishers@gmail.com

(She turned; I saw her turning)

First Edition: 2009

ISBN (10) : 8183520693

ISBN (13) : 9788183520690

Distributed by
VAIBHAV BOOK SERVICE
e-mail : vaibhavbookservice@gmail.com

Published by D.K. Jha for Mahaveer Publishers

Printed by Chaman Offset Printers, New Delhi

ACKNOWLEDGEMENT

For my parents, who always pinned their faith in me,
and never encroached on my freedom.

Mushtaq Ahmad

For my dear Baji and Attiqa, who brought me up and
sacrificed their every joy for me.

Nabi Nazeer

And finally to all our friends for their love and support.

Dedicated to crores of Musmads,
who are still waiting for their Fairynelos
in the hope that one day they will melt in their love.

FOREWORD

It was the day of judgement! Everybody was rubbing hands, waiting for his turn. The old acquaintances had become meaningless in the dreadful environment of the judgement day. Though stark naked, nobody was looking at the other as the sound of foreboding alarm was becoming louder and louder.

When Musmad was summoned before Allah, he was immediately declared a virtuous soul. After congratulating Musmad, the angels clad him in green. Now Musmad looked as though he was a newly-crowned prince. Soon Fairynelo entered, hands clasped to her bosom. Angels stared at her in disbelief. If the angels were to give their verdict, they would have declared her sinless, but Allah sees only the beauty of virtue and so she was declared a guilty soul. Musmad did not look at her as he feared she might not recognise him. "I have got an apt punishment as I broke the heart of Musmad, who is now the heart-throb of fairies and might not recognise me," said Fairynelo, while being dragged away by the angels.

Musmad could not endure her ignominy and entreated Allah, "Stop them, my Allah. I love her; I do not need fairies. Throw me into hell if she is to be thrown in hell."

Allah decreed, "Stop and let her go with Musmad."

Fairynelo went over to Musmad and said, "Let me expiate my sins, my love, but wait for me on the bank of the milky stream until I come back."

Musmad replied sobbingly, "But I will be forlorn without you."

"No, my love, you are to exhibit indomitable fortitude as we are to relish the moments of love together," said Fairynelo encouragingly to Musmad.

"The milky streams and honey brooks are meaningless to me without you and I cannot savour them," said Musmad, while sobbing his heart out.

"No, my love, do not say this. When you go by the milky steam, drink its milk as it will slake the thirst of your love in the sizzling heat of hell. When you happen to pass by the honey brook, savour its honey as it will soothe the burning throat of your beloved. Promise me, you will stay blissfully happy until my return," begged Fairynelo of Musmad.

"I promise, but when will you come? " asked Musmad.

"Soon, very soon," said Fairynelo while walking away.

"After two months, after two months," suggested Musmad deliberately so that Fairynelo would reply, "Yes, my love, after two months."

But Fairynelo replied, "Soon my love, soon." Her voice soon got lost in the distance.

Everybody wept at this moving sight. Allah ordered the angles to stop crying but after some time, Allah turned around and wiped away his own tears and ordered, "Call the next."

CONTENTS

Foreword 7

1. Entrance to the Mosque 11
2. The Parsimonious Mothers 17
3. The Reverie 25
4. The Golden Daughters 35
5. The Vanquished King 51
6. The Prophet of Doom 63
7. Love Rituals 69
8. The King of Goodbye 87
9. The Cremation 97

1

Entrance to the Mosque

It had snowed all through the night. A black puppy with bleary eyes walked on the snowy road at dawn, looking around as though experiencing the icy chill of winter for the first time. Suddenly it somersaulted over the fluffy snow. After tormenting itself, it lay on its back, panting heavily but in sensuous ecstasy, which was hard to comprehend and impossible to explain. Snowflakes descended, some here, some there, and some straight into the poor puppy's eyes. Badgered by the snowflakes, it stood up and started sniffing at the snow, as though searching for its lost bone. Suddenly it stumbled over something, the movement of which not only startled it, but also coerced it to flee away, barking.

A seven-year-old boy sat up from his sprawled position, muttering, "Mad puppy has spoiled all my clothes and almost took the life out of me". The stumbling block in the path of the black puppy was a naive little boy. But what was he doing there at the unearthly hour, sitting on a mound of snow in the freezing month of January? After brushing crumbs of snow from his sweater, the little boy, whose name was Musmad, peered at the man, standing on the third step of the mosque's staircase. The man beamed at him and lowered his eyelids, as if beckoning him to 'start'. Musmad quickly took off his right shoe and hurled it away. With a sigh and very reluctantly, he placed his right foot on the snow. The snow melted under his foot, sending its searingly cold, obnoxious tentacles into his being. A wave of pang ran through his body, which eventually culminated into a desire to pull back his foot. Pulling back his right foot brought him an ephemeral respite. After a brief pause, he gathered the shattered courage to drop his left foot on the goose-flesh-inducing snow. However, this time he kept his left foot steady until it went numb. The numbness that made him oblivious of the world around, the numbness that brought tears into his eyes, the numbness that was a souvenir of his victory. Musmad stood up and marched towards the man on the stairs and said, "Oh, my master, see, I have done as you said. See, I can walk barefoot on snow."

Master Shamag had long hair worn in filthy braids, beard unkempt, moustache half in mouth, chewing tobacco that had dribbled through his beard. Hair had poked out of his nostrils and had formed an intricate network with the moustache, presenting a picture of repugnance. After a brief pause, Shamag said to Musmad, "You have a long way to go to be a consummate mad. Your madness will be put to test time and again, as feigning madness is difficult than being really mad. If the underlying secret of your phony madness is exposed to the people of Heavel, you will be proscribed from taking refuge in the mosque," pointed out Master Shamag.

Master Shamag grabbed Musmad by hand and clambered over the sharp precipice. They sat down cross-legged, facing each other. "I am Shamag. I have brought you here to teach you the four doctrines behind feigning madness.

Doctrine 1: Feel the pain, but never wince.

Doctrine 2: Rave...Rave...and rave, but rave to yourself.

Doctrine 3: Eat the leftovers of everyone; even of the animals.

Doctrine 4: Never take a bath. Let the hair grow and filth accumulate in the eaves of nails and the well of navel."

Shamag explained the doctrines of madness to Musmad as though a professional teacher was giving tips to his devoted pupil for an oncoming examination.

The mosque in Heavel was open to all for worship during the day, but it was a safe haven for insanes at night. A surreal wetness clouded the eyes of Musmad, which only Master Shamag could comprehend because he himself had been through the same plight. The Master knew that whatever he had taught Musmad was but a bagatelle price to stay alive. He felt no qualms at teaching Musmad the doctrines of feigning madness and neither did he feel ashamed of doing so because after all, his endeavours were aimed at ensuring Musmad's survival. For a boy who was an orphan, homeless and above all ostracised, the man like Shamag was a prophet despite the smudged filth on his hands, which could make anyone retch.

After roaming over every nook and cranny of Heavel day in and day out, they would return back to the mosque at dusk, exhausted and listless.

2

The Parsimonious Mothers

Musmad was seven-years old when his parents were killed, changing his exuberance into taciturnity. Master Shamag was the first person to teach him to walk barefoot on the snowy and rough roads of Heavel, whose roughness transformed the flaccid skin of his bare feet into calloused and coarse sores. People hurled stones at Musmad as though he was a statue of devil and stoning him washed off their sins. Musmad was the only cherub and son of his parents, who left him alone and without armour in a battlefield but with a naked sword of helplessness to fight the battle of life. Poor Musmad was vanquished in the battle of life, as he was not a virtuoso in the swordsmanship of hypocrisy. Barbaric demagogues of Heavel with their swords of hypocrisy sharpened to the hilt, chopped off the little delicate fluffy wings of the cherub, who had yet to learn flapping. Musmad was bludgeoned to set off on a journey of madness, which culminated in an equivocal ocean of pure love and affection. Musmad would sometimes sit on the coarse roads of Heavel and wish if he had a sister or brother, he would not feel so forlorn in the gloom of Heavel.

Master Shamag was his only companion and teacher, who did not teach him to read the books of science or to solve the problems of calculus, but taught him the doctrines of madness and pedagogy of feigning madness. When children of Musmad's age were decorating their juvenile dreams, Musmad would clamber over the precipice, overlooking the cemetery, the home of his parents. He would sit there for hours, staring pleadingly at the graves of his parents. Though Musmad had a herd of relatives, none came forward to adopt him; none came to offer refuge to a young sapling of lily, which developed into a spiky cactus in the impoverished soil of selfishness. If Musmad had been adopted, he could have become a doctor, a writer, or a leader. If a young sapling of lily had been nourished and watered properly, it would have developed into a complete and beautiful lily, which would fill a whole nation with its fragrance and soothe the bleary eyes of the poor by its soft petals. But the young sapling had by now grown into a fully developed cactus, whose spikes stung everybody who came in contact with them; even the cactus itself.

We have not been able to comprehend why people cultivate cactus for ornamentation, when its spikes sting? How can an obnoxious cactus be used for ornamentation? We think ugliness is an adverse definition of beauty and people love ugliness subliminally and equally as they love beauty, the only difference being that beauty is loved openly, while ugliness is loved subliminally. If ugliness were abolished from the world, beauty would lose its charm and intoxication. Only those can comprehend true beauty, who know how to love ugliness. Beauty is meaningless without ugliness. Ugliness is a leprous mother of beauty, who always hides her leprous face in a veil so that her gorgeous daughter, Beauty, may not feel embarrassed before her ravishing friends. Musmad was a soulful poet who sang real songs of beauty in the streets of Heavel.

On Friday, Musmad would sit beside his mother's grave and reminisce over every moment that he had spent in her soft lap. He would level the earth of his mother's grave and weed out thorny bushes. When strong arms of madness grabbed Musmad, he forgot his mother and neglected the grave which soon got covered with thorny bushes and weeds.

Though Musmad forgot his mother, she always prayed for his well-being, even in the darkness of her grave. Long and deep sighs emanating from Musmad's mother's grave could be heard by the darkness and stillness of night only. The voice, which, if the people of Heavel had heard, they would have thrashed themselves to death for ostracising the cherub of heaven.

Mothers never stop loving their adorable children, but are very parsimonious with their love as they lavish it only over their own children. Mother is the goddess of love, owning a fathomless ocean of affection but its water is only for her own children. The ocean, whose water cannot slake the thirst of the poor, is like a glass of water with a dead rat in it, whose water retches even a desperately thirsty man. Allah has bestowed an infinite ocean of love on mothers to slake the thirst of every child, but selfish mothers spare that for their children only. On the Day of Judgement, Allah will ask mothers of Heavel, "I had bestowed on you the bottomless ocean of love. What did you do to it?"

Mothers will say, "Our Lord, we slaked the thirst of the children."

Allah will continue, "Which children?"

Mothers will reply hesitantly, "Our own children, Allah."

Allah will shake his head despondently and say, "Oh mothers of Heavel, if you had been generous with your love, children like Musmad would not have remained deprived of the cool shade of motherhood."

No mother of Heavel ever gave Musmad a few tiny drops of her love; no mother of Heavel ever kissed Musmad on cheeks and patted his head and said, "Musmad, what happened if your mother passed away? I am your mother; my warm lap will protect you against the chill of winter. I am always with you in your triumphs and failures."

When life becomes unbearable, man longs and prays for death. Despite being tormented by every moment of life for no obvious reason, Musmad would roam every night in Heavel and stop at the cemetery, situated at the backside of the mosque and ask the forsaken corpses in forsaken graves, covered with spiky bushes, "Do you find comfort in the dark abode of the graves?"

A corpse of a young man would conjure up and reply, "Yes sir, the tranquillity of graves defies explanation, and its comfort is exemplary."

Soon another corpse of an old man would appear, and say, "My son, I was a school teacher. The mosquitoes of wealth and flies of fame never let me sleep on my soft, luxurious bed. They incited me to hoard more and more wealth and inveigled me into exalting more and more fame. They never let me teach my students the songs of heavenly love. I was a pedagogue, who could never make his home in the soft hearts of his students. Teachers like me are responsible for the plight of orphans like you. Now I am expiating my sins in the darkness of the grave, whose serenity and peace are epitomes of comfort."

When the old teacher completed, a flock of tall slender corpses of middle-aged men with long white beards conjured up from their graves, which were in a single row, and said in one voice, "We are responsible for your plight, as we stabbed the society in the back with a rusty knife of phony virtuousness. We kept on rolling it till all the blood of morality and modesty flowed out, and the bloodless pale body of society crumbled down with a crash. Without taking any pity, we sold its dead organs and went on pilgrimage. Orphans and proletariats did come when we left for pilgrimage, but those fools did not know the body, which is fed on pork, cannot feel agony at the sufferings of the destitute. Oh Musmad, our son, we are not worthy of your pardon and don't forgive us even if you are asked to by our posterity as we want to atone for our sins in this abode of grave, whose comfort is worthy to be coveted."

Every person savours slumber in the serenity of the grave. The virtuous souls are served by fairies and angels for keeping their hems pious while crossing the dirty sea of guilt in the world, while the guilty souls desperately try to rub off the stains of guilt on their hems with the soap of expiation. Rubbing off each stain brings them ecstasy of heaven. If comfort is brought by virtuousness, then expiation of sins brings ecstasy, and both are duo attributes of the grave.

3

The Reverie

Spring, the season of tiny raindrops, makes the blossoms bloom on trees and produces a bizarre feeling in young hearts when the raindrops slowly seep through the minute pores of their clothes, and spread their wet wings on the skin and tickle every desire, which cajoles them to get lost in a reverie and hum softly while walking slowly in the relentless rain. The raindrops not only drenched Musmad and tickled his desires, hidden deep inside his being, but also washed off the obstinate grime from his calloused skin and long hair worn in plaits. Musmad leaned back against a boulder, staring into space and blinking his eyes as the stubborn raindrops surreptitiously carved their way into his arid eyes. He could hear the musical sound of the raging torrent in the deserted river, which separated Heavel from the hustle and bustle of the town. The high and low musical notes of the torrent were complemented by the soulful music of a sudden gust of wind, in which the orchestra of young sizzling raindrops joined to play the percussion. Leaves played their respective flutes: some applied a whole note, some played at minim note. A soulful song composed by Allah, sung by the wind and orchestrated by the rain, was played to celebrate the advent of teens of Musmad, who himself was oblivious of coming manhood, knocking at the door of his boyhood. Though Musmad did not know, he had become twelve years, eleven months and thirty days old. Still restlessness grew in him as the last day of his boyhood passed.

As the dusk spread its dark, heavy iron wings, Musmad started feeling youth's bud sprouting from the seed of boyhood. The bud grew with mounting darkness and triggered in him the weirdest feelings, which he could not fathom. At 11:59 p.m., Musmad was at the brink of adolescence. Oblivious of coming manhood, Musmad instinctively preened himself to welcome youth when the clock of his heart ticked one...two...three...twenty.... thirty...forty...fifty...fifty-nine...and finally chimed midnight.

But he was lost in a reverie and saw her coming out of the heart of the river, wet and hot at the same time. She was drenched in the sweat of her own modesty as clinging clothes revealed the contours of her body. Though Musmad knew Fairynelo for a long time, he had never been lured to her. He would often see her going to school with her friends but had never felt as he was feeling now. These feelings were strange to him like a father to a newly born baby. When he could not comprehend these feelings, he asked darkness, "Why am I thinking about Fairynelo and not about her friend Qazia Shams when she is more ravishing than Fairynelo? Please tell, please tell me."

Darkness just smiled under her dark veil and mumbled to herself, 'Really Musmad is now a consummate mad. Foolish Musmad, mad Musmad.'

Musmad wept and sobbed all through the dark night, occasionally plucking his hair. Entrance into teenage had turned him frantic. At dawn, he fell into sleep, yet reminiscing about Fairynelo and muttering her name, "Fairynelo.... Fairynelo.... Fairynelo.... Fairynelo...." Now reigned complete silence except for the rain, which continuously sang lullaby for the teen-turned-man. Teenage is the age of getting lost in reverie and seeing the queen of one's heart in everything and everywhere.

Musmad got up early, went to the washroom, closing the door behind. After pondering for a while, he took out a jagged piece of mirror from his pocket and squatted down, leaning against the wall. He raised the mirror, looking straight into his eyes in the mirror. There was no glistening, no shine; the blizzard of time had blown all life away from his eyes, leaving behind an ugly image of Musmad, which could only torment his own eyes, because thorns are not made for soothing. Musmad raised the mirror slowly until his eyes fell on his long filthy braids of hair, the abode of lice.

Musmad promptly lowered the mirror and stopped at his face, the grime of which nauseated him. Without thinking even for a while, Musmad closed his eyes and mumbled, 'Musmad, you have to groom yourself. You have to bring life in your eyes, shine on face and look handsome if you want to get Fairynelo.' Musmad at once stripped himself naked, took a piece of used soap from the mosque's windowsill and began to scrub himself vigorously. He scrubbed the filth from his skin until blood started spurting out. Indeed love makes a man fool. Love is the mother of desire, which induces a man to preen and bedeck himself for his beloved. Love entices a man to look into the mirror and assess the oddities on his face. Love makes a man mad. After having a bath, Musmad looked again into the mirror and mumbled, 'Now, I have to clean them,' beaming as though he was showing his bloody pale gums to his mother.

The months of spring passed but Musmad never saw Fairynelo in these humid months, which had aroused the spring of love in his life; months, which had carved love on his petrified heart. Musmad's eyes yearned to catch a glimpse of Fairynelo, because they desperately needed her glimpse just like a deep laceration needs a prompt treatment lest it develops infection. When his forbearance fell over the verge of his endurance, he decided to go to Fairynelo's home.

At noon he loudly battered the main gate, but no one came out. He bawled and battered the gate more furiously.

Fairynelo was studying for her forthcoming pre-medical exams. The battering noise distracted her each time she tried to concentrate. At last her patience gave way and she stood up angrily, went over to the gate and asked, "Who is there?"

Fairynelo's voice, though shrill, brought immediate relief to Musmad, alleviating his heart like a baby's, whose hunger pangs find relief on sucking the dry nipples of his mother's breasts. Fairynelo opened the door with quaking hands and saw Musmad standing at the gate like a statue. She sighed and said, "You took the life out of me. Could you not wait until I opened the door? Stupid! Mad! Go away and come later. There is no one at home." Slamming the door angrily behind her, she rushed inside. Strangely enough, perhaps at her whim, she returned to the gate after half an hour and peeped through the chink. She found Musmad rooted there with tears trickling down his eyes. When love is bilateral, it is the most exhilarating experience but when it is unilateral, it becomes the most tormenting feeling.

Summer gave way to autumn, the trees shed their leaves, but Musmad did not stop loving Fairynelo. He would always sit on the embankment of the river, legs hanging over, and look pleadingly at leafless trees and bare stones as though beseeching them to go and call Fairynelo. When Fairynelo did not come, he stood up and implored the plants, "Oh munificent plants, you produce food for everyone, irrespective of cast, colour, sanity and insanity. Cannot you go and tell Fairynelo that Musmad is waiting for her? Tell her, come before I die. But, how can you go? You do not have legs." Musmad knelt and turned to a dog to plead sobbingly, "You have the incredible power of sniffing; you can sniff the stink of my decaying heart. Go and tell Fairynelo, 'Come before Musmad's heart succumbs to the decay'." The dog just barked and slithered away.

Musmad slipped off the embankment and went sprawling on the dusty road. He wept and thrust the dusty road desperately. The wind, unable to bear his plight, sent a sudden gust, carrying the smell of Musmad to Fairynelo. As the wavy fingers of the wind touched Fairynelo's face, she said to her mother, "Mom, goodbye. I had better leave now lest I get late for my pre-medical exam."

The wind rushed back to whisper softly in Musmad's ears, 'Fool, get up; she is coming.'

Lovers have the instinct to forefeel the arrival of their beloved. Musmad quickly got up, ran to the river and splashed his face with its cold water, which brought some charm to his haggard face. He sat down on the last step of the staircase leading to the river, waiting for Fairynelo. Soon he heard the sound of approaching footsteps. The sound grew louder and louder as Fairynelo and her friends drew nearer. Fairynelo's friends boarded on the boat, waiting to take them across the river.

Although Heavel was connected to the town, both with the main bridge and a footbridge, the people of Heavel preferred to cross by boat as it not only saved time, but also eased their journey. As Fairynelo set her right foot on the boat, Musmad grabbed the hem of her gown, the cache encasing her golden body. Fairynelo, thinking that her gown had snagged on something, turned to look back. She saw Musmad clutching the hem of her gown. Fairynelo gently disembarked from the boat, and squatted down, facing Musmad. Taking his hands in her hands, she looked into his eyes. "What can I do for my little angel?" asked Fairynelo.

"Just love me until time ceases to exist," pleaded Musmad. Musmad had never talked to anybody like this before.

The people of Heavel would say, "Musmad has mystical powers; he can prophesy anyone's future. Whosoever does Musmad stop is showered with good fortune."

Fairynelo wanted to slap Musmad on the face when he asked her to love him, but stopped, as she thought, 'Musmad has mystical powers. If I scold him, he will curse me with bad luck.' So she replied with an ostentatious smile, "Okay, I will, but you have to promise you will love me until I ask you to love."

Foolish Musmad impetuously nodded his head, little realising what he had promised.

"I have to go now as I am getting late for my exams. Just pray for me that I should qualify in my pre-medical exams," said Fairynelo hastily, as her friends were waiting impatiently for her in the boat. But Musmad held on to the hem, which was his only saviour in the tempest of life. It was the hem around which he had woven his unfeasible dreams.

Fairynelo cajoled Musmad into relinquishing her hem by saying, "My little cute angel, am I not getting late? Do you want your Fairynelo to fail in the exams? Let me go this time. I promise to spend a whole day with you tomorrow." So saying, she ruffled his unkempt hair with her soft hands.

Musmad slowly and reluctantly let the hem go off. She embarked on the boat with a sigh of relief, thinking she was fortunate enough to have been blessed by a mystic. Musmad was there long after Fairynelo's departure, thinking she loved him. Musmad misconstrued Fairynelo's sympathy as love, while Fairynelo misconstrued Musmad as an angel of fate, but both were happy.

4

The Golden Daughters

Musmad was left to starve to death. For the past two days, he had not been given a morsel to eat. The grim walls of the lockup coupled with its blood-curdling darkness were not alien to Musmad, as he had slept in their laps since childhood. He was too frail to stand. No one could gauge his agony and suffering in the gloom of the jail. He would occasionally rave and rant, but most of the times he slept, trying to relive his dream about Fairynelo. When he could not dream, he would close his eyes, clench his teeth, and say desperately, "This time, I must see her." Musmad's only companions in jail were the taciturn darkness and the deathly silence, which are companions of every insane, because the insane make those his companions which are abhorred by the sane.

At dusk of the third day, policemen opened the door not to serve food, but to incarcerate another victim of the sanes. A twenty-year-old boy, looking more like a gentleman than a callous criminal, was frog-marched into the jail by two corpulent policemen. The boy remained reticent for a long time. At 9:30 p. m., the frail Musmad lit a candle, the light of which uncovered an insane Musmad to a sane Nasane. "What crime have you committed?" Musmad asked Nasane.

Silence...deathly silence...

"Have you perpetrated a murder, or a rape, or arson?" continued Musmad.

After a deep silence, Nasane replied, "Love...love.... yes, I have perpetrated the crime of falling in love. Yes, an orphan has dared to transgress the boundaries drawn by earthly gods, who petrify the hearts of their daughters and leave no space for us in their petrified hearts."

Little did Nasane know that the alter ego of his was present before him in the form of Musmad.

There are crores of Musmads, some sane, some insane, but all are hanged on the gallows of unsuccessful love by the hangmen, who are idols of avarice and fathers of the golden daughters; the golden daughters, who yearn for lovers with golden hearts; the golden daughters, who can doll up the bride of life, but cannot bring smile on her dry withered lips; the golden daughters, who are devoid of love, the most precious gift of the universe. Madmen are mad for they still love the golden daughters, because love is not blind but bestows heavenly eyes on lovers, enabling them to see the utopia and beguiles them into believing that one day the golden daughters would melt in their love.

At 11:00 p.m., the door of the lockup was reopened by some policemen, who called out, "Who is Nasane? Your sister has come to meet you."

Nasane hurried to the door, whose cold bars he could not cross.

"How is my son?" asked Nasane's sister, with tears in her eyes, which she was desperately trying to hold back, so that Nasane's courage would not melt at her helpless tears.

"I am fine. Do not worry about me," replied Nasane smilingly, pretending to be happy. "You should not have come here at this time; it is too late," said Nasane.

"Everything at home was reminding me of you. When I sat down to have meal, I could not, as I knew my son was hungry. I have come with food for my son," replied Nasane's sister with a sigh.

"But I am not hungry. Please take this back."

"Did the police beat you?" asked Nasane's sister. Nasane shook his head, but bruises and lacerations belied him.

"I will get you out tomorrow, my son. You just don't worry," said the sister, trying to console him.

"But how, but how? But how?" They both cried and burst into tears, as if their dam of tears had burst at their helplessness. Musmad too wept in the darkness.

Nasane's sister went away, leaving food for the two hungry lovers.

At 1:00 a.m., when everybody was savouring sleep, Musmad coaxed Nasane into having some food. After having supper, Nasane asked, "What offence have you committed?"

"Fairynelo was with her father, when I went over to her and asked to spend the day with me, as she had promised. But her father gathered a huge mob, which stripped me naked and painted me with black smoke. The others beat me and placed a wreath of dilapidated shoes around my neck. Later, Fairynelo's father handed me over to the police," said Musmad, narrating his plight to Nasane, as though a grandfather was narrating a fairytale to his grandson.

Musmad got up and took two hallucinogen-filled cigarettes from his pocket. He lit one himself and offered another to Nasane, but he refused.

"Oh, my friend, this cigarette will open up a new world for you, which you could have never conceived. But I don't puff on this cigarette for that heavenly world; puffing enables me to see my Fairynelo. This cigarette has a magical pencil, which draws my Fairynelo on the board of the smoke. Look, I will show you how," said Musmad, taking a long puff on the cigarette. Raising his right hand, he said, "See, see my friend, the magical pencil has drawn my Fairynelo's tresses, whose wavy locks are flying with the waft of the breeze, filling my breath with the smell of her breath. The magical pencil is so naughty that it has drawn her drowsy eyes before the sharp contours of her body. Oh, my friend of one night, these are not only beautiful eyes, but also two magical mirrors made by the supreme artist of the universe, in which I see my dishevelled countenance look beautiful. Okay, goodnight my friend, I am to go now, as Fairynelo is waiting to take me in her arms." So saying, Musmad flopped down, muttering, "Fairynelo... Fairynelo...Fairynelo," for some time before dozing off to deep.

Next morning, Mr. Nawani, father of Nasane's beloved came to intimidate Nasane. "You cannot come out of here; you will rot here," threatened Mr. Nawani. Nasane merely lifted his weary eyelids, but said nothing.

Nasane owned a teastall; he fell in love with Mr. Nawani's daughter, Kissbery. One day, Nasane wrote a love letter to Kissbery to express his love, but Kissbery handed over the letter to her father, and soon Nasane reached behind the bars. Poor Nasane didn't know that a teastallholder is made to serve tea, not be served the tea of love. Mr. Nawani humiliated Nasane; he even threw expletives and obscenities at his late parents. Nasane listened to the abuses and obscenities threw by Mr. Nawani just as a submissive slave listens to his master. Occasionally he would lift and rub his eyelids, but said nothing to Mr. Nawani.

"You have only one way to come out of here. You desist from harassing my daughter and apologise for your indecent act," suggested Mr. Nawani. Nasane was lacerated with the spear of humiliation. Eventually he succumbed to his helplessness and apologised to Mr. Nawani.

Sane lovers can be prevented from loving golden daughters by using the weapons of humiliation and intimidation, but how will fathers of golden daughters stop insane lovers, like Musmad, who are immune to humiliation and intimidation because man cannot humiliate those who have been humiliated by time?

At 11:00 in the morning, Nasane was acquitted. Musmad hugged him and said, "Do not lose hope; everything will go your way."

"I have now realised that orphans do not have a love story," replied Musmad and departed.

When he reached the threshold of the lockup, Musmad called out from behind, "Some love stories form to be talked about, some to be tasted, some to be read. Yours too will form and all people will a give standing ovation, as you hug her with tears welled in both of your eyes at the verge of fall. Despite your frantic attempts to hold them back, they will dribble down. When she sees the falling tears, she will wipe them off, and look deep into your eyes. Then she will smile as though you were her son. Your love story is consummate and is made for a happy ending...Eyes-into-eyes ending...hug ending...marriage ending...arranged by angels ending...hosted by God ending...larger than life ending."

On hearing these words from Musmad, Nasane's dreary face glowed with joy. Two days later, Musmad too was acquitted.

Musmad could have entered on foot, but he crawled into the mosque so that the muck on the soles of his feet would not spoil the sacred carpet of the mosque. When he reached the centre of the mosque, he sat down cross-legged, keeping his hands under his feet. "It is true, my Allah; I have entered your home without having ablutions. I know it is a grave sin, which cannot be pardoned, but what can I do? I have never been taught how to have ablutions. I have heard, my Allah, that meaningless sins of meaningless men are not counted in the ledgers of heaven, so please forgive me," pleaded Musmad. "They beat me and don't let me see my Fairynelo, my Allah!" complained Musmad.

Musmad crawled to the window with the black pane and thought, 'This is a good vantage point to see Fairynelo without revealing myself. No one can see me through the black pane.'

Musmad watched Fairynelo come and watched her walk past, till she got lost in the distance. One glimpse of Fairynelo was not enough to prevent the painful and lingering death of his thirsty soul, the soul that was clamouring to see Fairynelo. Musmad crawled back to the door of the mosque, leading to the cemetery, to catch another glimpse of Fairynelo. He stopped at the threshold and addressed the graves, "Oh, the heaven-dwellers, give me the imprimatur to run over your graves, as these earth- dwellers do not let me see my love. They beat me, they curse me, they stone me."

Musmad then stepped gingerly on his mother's grave, the soil of which squelched, "May Allah bless you, my son." This squelch exhorted him to accelerate his walk into a run. He ran over the graves, through the bushes with thorns piercing the soles of his feet as serrated glass pieces stabbed the arches, making their way through the insteps. On reaching the other side of the cemetery, he saw Fairynelo standing outside the main entrance of her house, talking to her friends. Musmad, breathless, panting heavily, caught a blurred sight of Fairynelo through the salty drops of sweat, dribbling down his forehead into his arid eyes. Though engrossed in chatting with her friends, we don't know why, perhaps at her whim, she turned around, and saw Musmad lurking in the cemetery. As soon as Musmad saw her turning around, he stooped down to hide himself.

Fairynelo chuckled behind her hands, and said, "Fool! Look, look in the cemetery. Mad Musmad is watching us." When her friends turned to look, Musmad quickly hid himself behind the bushes. They all laughed until they became hysterical and tears sprouted in their eyes.

"She is happy; she is not angry with me. This means she will not tell her father that Musmad was watching her. This means she loves me," mumbled Musmad.

"I do not think Musmad is mad. At times he does not look mad. I think he is feigning madness," said Fairynelo to her friends.

"But he is so naive, so ingenuous. I would marry him, were he not mad or if I too were mad," replied Fairynelo's friend Qazia Shams. A wet wave of jealousy ran through Fairynelo's body, reviving the promising hopes in mad Musmad's heart; the wave that watered the withering bud of Musmad's love in Fairynelo's heart.

"I think it is too late; we should leave now," said Qazia Shams. As soon as Fairynelo closed the gate, Musmad went off, amply contended. That night he slept like a child with a coruscating smile on his lips, but Fairynelo couldn't sleep as memories of Musmad conjured up weird feelings in her, which she didn't want to comprehend.

Fairynelo was waiting in a long queue to submit her admission form when Iranzir walked past her. Not abruptly, but slowly she turned with the passing of Iranzir, as though a piece of paper was turning around in a whirlpool.

It was the happiest day in the life of Fairynelo, as she alone had qualified in the pre-medical examination among her friends, and her long-awaited dream of becoming a doctor was on the brink of completion. After submitting her admission form, she desperately looked around for Iranzir, whom she eventually found sitting and reading a book under the shade of a *chinar* tree. She went over to him and said hesitantly, "My grandmother believed in 'love at first sight' and my parents say that I am an alter ego of my grandmother."

Iranzir tried to stifle his smile, but failed when he heard the weirdest words of Fairynelo. Fairynelo was very friendly with her words and could say anything effortlessly. Though Iranzir was very shy, he gazed at Fairynelo, whose fair complexion and blonde tresses held back under a white scarf, tucked under her ears and tied under her chin with a golden tiepin, were enough to urge any poet to compose an ode. Fairynelo was waiting for Iranzir's reply when he stood up and said, "My grandfather believed in, 'one should marry the girl, who believes in love at first sight' and my parents too say that I can alter ego of my grandfather."

A smile of relief stretched Fairynelo's rosy lips, sending her heart racing. Then followed the meetings on sly between Iranzir and Fairynelo. They began spending every evening together ever since their first meeting. When their parents came to know about their love, they gave their consent for marriage without much ado.

Lovers often miss the beautiful days of togetherness by remaining tongue-tied. Cash...cash your dreams before they obscure in the distance.

* * *

Musmad was standing at the three-stepped stile, which led into a lush green lawn, whose fence had been painted and covered with blinking lights, conjuring up a surreal perception of day and night alternatively in every guest who came to attend the engagement party of Fairynelo and Iranzir. Not only the lawn, but also every nook and niche of Fairynelo's house had been painted and decorated with blinking lights to celebrate the betrothal of the young couple. When all the guests of and outside Heavel had arrived, Fairynelo, in a pink bridal dress and her face covered in a rosy veil, was escorted out by Qazia Shams to the lawn, where Iranzir was waiting with a throbbing heart. As Iranzir slipped the ring on to the ring finger of Fairynelo amidst the huge clapping, Musmad clasped his fingers, closed his eyes and prayed, "Please, my Allah, make that ominous engagement ring to get lost!"

Alas, when he opened his eyes, the guests were greeting the newly-engaged couple. As Fairynelo and Iranzir went inside hand in hand, Musmad besought the obsequious servants, "Let me in. I know she is being coerced into marrying this doctor. She loves me, I know." But the sycophant servants did not let him cross the mahogany stile of his dreams and pushed him out.

The sky raged when Musmad was thrown out. It started shooting pellets of raindrops, piercing the delicate leaves and leaving them in tatters. Heavel had never before witnessed such relentless rain, which not only washed off the newly painted walls of Fairynelo's house, but also turned the blissful environment into deathly silence. The storm did not want to stay behind in devastating Heavel for persecuting their companion, so it came with its army of hurricane, which not only knocked down trees and electricity poles, but also blew away thatches. The whole of Heavel lay in ruins, as though bandits had rampaged through it. When the guests were rushing out to return to their homes, Musmad squatted down under a big *chinar* tree, burying his head in the gorge of his arms. The storm buffeted the raindrops, which slipped down the leaves and drenched Musmad. But he did not move as though incantation and the spell of raindrops had petrified him into a sitting statue of love. After a long time, when the rain had stopped, Musmad raised his head, but it was virtually impossible to judge whether the trickling drops from his face were tears or raindrops!

Fairynelo and Qazia Shams were going to town to buy trousseau and bridal jewellery when Musmad confronted them, saying, "Look, look, my fair complexion and good-looking face. Am I not more handsome than that doctor? See, see, filth is no more on my skin or under the eaves of my nails, which I clipped off yesterday. I am taller than that doctor, whose short stature does not complement you. If you say, I will get my haircut, and buy some new clothes. I will start doing some work, and earn a lot of money for you. I will keep you always happy. Will you marry me now?"

Fairynelo and Qazia Shams listened stupefied to Musmad's silly words, waiting to make their escape. When Musmad did not give way, Fairynelo shouted, "Will you please give way? I thought you were a vitreous boy, but you are a devil of devils, who should be beaten to death lest you mar the entire society. I do not love you. How dare you even think that I love you? When you grabbed my hem, I thought you were my well-wisher and wanted my success, but you have defamed me instead. I love only Iranzir. You are a fool, who construed my sympathy as love."

When Musmad heard Fairynelo calling him a fool, he slowly gave them way. He was there with tears in his eyes, long after Fairynelo went, but this time tears forgot to trickle down, as he was lost in reckoning who is the real Fairynelo? One, who promised, "I will love you until time ceases to exist." Or one, who insisted, "You are a fool, who construed my sympathy as love."

Fairynelo's historic marriage was scheduled on Sunday of next month, but the hour-hand of the clock of Musmad's doom doubled its speed and soon the Sunday of Fairynelo's marriage arrived. The marriage, which plunged Musmad into the abyss of despair; the marriage, which marked the union of Fairynelo and Iranzir, and the lingering death of Musmad. Everybody came to the marriage. Musmad too came, not to savour the feast, but to catch a glimpse of Fairynelo for the last time. When the hands and nails of Fairynelo were being manicured, Musmad was biting his nails in wait for a last glimpse of Fairynelo. When the feet and toenails of Fairynelo were undergoing pedicure, Musmad was rubbing his feet in the dust of despair. When mascara was being put on her eyelashes, Musmad was drenching his eyelashes in tears. When Fairynelo was waiting for the arrival of her groom, Musmad was playing the foolish game of three pebbles. He closed his eyes, and said, "If my finger falls on the middle pebble, then I will see my Fairynelo." The finger fell, not on the first, not on the third, but on the middle pebble on which all hopes of Musmad depended. He jumped in the air with overwhelming joy.

Soon the valedictory time came. Fairynelo was sent off with her groom by showering red, yellow, and purple petals of rose mingled with toffees of varied kind, over them. When the children and the madmen of Heavel were engrossed in jostling for toffees, Musmad was trying frantically to catch one glimpse of Fairynelo, who was surrounded by people. When Musmad could not see her, he stood on tiptoe and caught a glimpse of Fairynelo while she was climbing the back seat of the car. The car gathered speed, first slowly, and then fast. Musmad walked behind and soon his walk turned into a run. The car disappeared in the distance, and Musmad knelt down and cried on the bend of the road, which obscured Heavel from the rest of the world. “Oh Allah, by taking away the only reason to live, you have made me a complete destitute,” wailed Musmad.

The people of Heavel said that Fairynelo did not look back on leaving Heavel, but Musmad said, “I swear, she looked back at me when the car reached the bend of the road. These fools did not see her turning.” Ever since the departure of Fairynelo, Musmad would mumble, “I saw her turning. She turned; I saw her turning.”

of the road, which obscured Heaven from the rest of the world. Oh, Allah, by taking away the only reason to live you have made me a complete destitute," wailed Mumtaz.

The mourners of Haveli [illegible] appeared [illegible] of Paving Heaven. But Mumtaz said, "[illegible] the ear [illegible] the end of the road. The [illegible] did [illegible]?" [illegible] Mumtaz would mumble, "I saw her turning. She turned; I saw her turning."

5

The Vanquished King

Musmad clambered over the precipice, the abode of a cold breeze and surreal solitude. He sat down on a big flat rock and took out a dirty matchbox out of his pocket. Without thinking even for a while, he set his hair on fire and dropped his eyelids just as withered leaves fall from their mother branches during autumn. He sat placidly while his hair burned, as though getting physical pleasure from the searing heat of the fire, as though not sensing the burning sensation. Grazing cows and buffaloes watched the burning hair of Musmad with fear, but when he didn't move, they thought a withered bush was burning and went back to grazing. Musmad heard neither the shrieks of the bursting lice nor the yell of the dying sensory receptors in his skin. Some lice were massacred, some lost their abode, but Musmad lost his last acquaintance with sanity.

When the cowgirl took the cows back home, Musmad's braids were still smouldering. After burning his eyelashes and eyebrows, Musmad threw the matchbox down the precipice and viciously rubbed the blisters on his head until they burst open, and sap dribbled all along the face. A waft of smoke did rise, but it soon got mixed in the air. The stench of burning did spread, but it was soon blown away by the cold breeze. Nobody came to know that Musmad had lost touch with sanity. Though Musmad looked handsome even in tattered clothes, now he looked like a scary ugly vampire from hell.

Musmad stood up, scratching his wet head. He now looked an entirely different Musmad. The old Musmad but with a new grace; old eyes, but a new way of seeing things; old ears, but which could hear beyond the power of hearing. Allah confers new sensory powers on the insane, which are completely alien to the sanę world. Musmad looked at Heavel spurting its usual fumes of avarice. His honed ears heard the clamour of impetuous fathers, coming from Heavel, who were exhorting their sons and daughters to double their speed of ambition to become a doctor, an engineer, or an IAS officer. Suddenly Musmad raved in a musical tone, "Hear...hear these impetuous fathers say, 'yes I know my son. You can become an IAS officer, as you are my blood. Don't let me down, my son, run fast.... run fast, success is waiting for you.' Alas, despite their cheering remarks, their sons have fallen down. Alas, sons have fallen down in their endeavor to run fast. See...see, the selfish fathers have run to their sons, and are rebuking them, 'you have mingled my respect in mud. I splurge so much money on you. I forgive you this time, but next time, I want to see you on top of the IAS list.' Hi...hi... Poor sons...poor sons...poor sons!" The breathless Musmad sat down panting heavily. After taking a brief pause, he stood up and raved again in a singing tone, "Shame...shame on the apprehensive fathers of golden daughters, who say, 'you have to run fast, my daughter. You have to become a doctor lest no handsome guy will marry you, and you will grow into a spinster' Shame...shame...Iranzir is a doctor; Fairynelo is a doctor. Doctors will marry doctors; the unemployed will marry the unemployed; the ugly will marry the ugly; but who will marry me? Fairynelo, yes...yes, Fairynelo. But, she has gone!" Whosoever passed by, watched Musmad rant but none could make sense of his raving. Musmad raved and ranted until it got stark dark, and then fell asleep in the lap of precipice.

Next morning, Musmad was awakened by the motherly touch of Master Shamag. When Musmad saw Master Shamag, he hugged him and wept like a child. Musmad had not seen Master Shamag for ten years. Master Shamag had grown old, and looked very gaunt. "Where have you been, my master? They beat me and parted me from my Fairynelo. I wept a lot on the bend of the road, but she turned; I saw her turning," explained Musmad, incoherently.

Master Shamag realised that Musmad had stepped into the enlightened world of insanity. He held him close to his chest and said placatingly, "My son, I have lived a long life, but I was not as lucky as you, as I could not transgress the boundaries of sanity, as I could not step into the world of insanity and fantasy. Though I am in tattered clothes, though I am covered with filth, I still am as sane as the people of Heavel. I still feign madness despite my lifelong attempts to become a consummate mad. When I was a little boy, my grandfather used to narrate to me the story of two brothers, whose names were Sane and Insane. Insane was ten minutes older than Sane. Their mother was blind, deaf and dumb. Sane was also blind, deaf and dumb like his mother. Sane didn't know that Insane was his elder brother, and he believed that his mother had only one breast, which was meant for him. When they were six-months old, they used to suck the two different nipples of their mother's breasts. Sane never came to know that Insane was his elder brother, though Insane tried a lot to convey that he was his elder brother and that their mother had two breasts, one for Sane and one for Insane. Had Sane not been blind, deaf and dumb, he would have known that he had a knowledgeable brother Insane, who was sucking the other nipple of their mother's breast. My son, all people are born sane, but only a few lucky ones touch the zenith of insanity and you are one among them. Allah has conferred this boon of insanity on you, my son. Let us prostrate before Him and thank Him for this precious boon."

Master Shamag prostrated before Allah and besought, while closing his eyes, "Make my death easy; save me from lingering death, my Allah."

Following Master Shamag, Musmad too prostrated before Allah, but asked for nothing. When Master Shamag raised his head, blood was spurting from his mouth, but he made no attempt to stop the flow as though it meant nothing to him. Master Shamag prostrated again, and prayed, "Musmad is the vanquished king of love, who has lost his kingdom and Queen Fairynelo in the draught of fate. Return to the vanquished king his lost kingdom and queen, my Allah."

Musmad too prostrated again, but this time he said, "She turned; I saw her turning."

Master Shamag and Musmad remained in prostration for an hour. They were numb in prostration as though a bizarre serenity had embraced them, as though they had achieved real happiness of life. A cold breeze did come, but Master Shamag was no more. His body rolled down the precipice with a slight nudge of the breeze. It rained and rained that day. Why? We do not know. After three days, Master Shamag was buried in the bosom of the earth, next to the graves of Musmad's parents.

Heavel was a small village in Paindise state of Polingual. Paindise was famous for its mystique landscapes and four non-twin seasons, luring tourists from every nook and cranny of the world. Paindise had always been the apple of dispute between Polingual and its neighboring country, Marionet. This dispute not only vandalised Paindise, but also paralysed the developing Polingual and Marionet, making the lives of the people in both the countries miserable. Sisters lost their brothers, mothers their sons, and children their parents in the neglected fire of ego and ignorance. Musmad was a victim of the same neglected fire of ignorance.

When the people of Heavel had nothing special to do, they would ridicule Musmad. Children would say, "We have heard Fairynelo didn't look at you when she left Heavel. Is it true?"

Musmad would just mumble, "She turned; I saw her turning. I swear by Allah, she turned; I saw her turning."

Youths would tease, "The government has decreed to reunite parted lovers. Now you will soon be with your Fairynelo."

Musmad would beg of them, "Is it true? Please tell me, will Fairynelo come back?"

The elderly people would say, "We met Fairynelo yesterday; she was inquiring about you. She told us to tell Musmad to have a bath every day. We will tell him that Musmad does not bathe daily if you do not sing a song for us."

Musmad would sing with a lisp,

Paindise will be green,
Heavel will be serene,
When the pure stream of light will be seen.

Mothers, more than orphans can desire,
Love and affection shall be ours upon that day,
When the pure stream of light will be seen.
Shackles of ignorance will be broken,
Yokes of slavery will be thrown.
Our minds will be free upon that day,
When the pure stream of light will be seen.
Poor will ask for wealth,
Rich will ask for health,
I will ask for my Fairynelo upon that day,
When the pure stream of light will be seen.

Fairynelo's parents were excited as Fairynelo was visiting them with her husband, Doctor Iranzir for the first time after marriage. Doctor Iranzir was an easy-going person, whose insouciance was beyond reproach. Iranzir was a submissive young man, whose submission always dominated assertion. Iranzir never had any altercation or discord with anybody. Even when someone tried to be bellicose with him, he would invariably greet with a deathless smile, which was the souvenir of his generosity and composure. People would say, "Allah has conferred beautiful Fairynelo on Iranzir as a gift for his humility."

Fairynelo was a professional doctor and a pragmatic woman, who not only believed in seeing things with her own eyes, but also in winning the hearts of the people with love and affection. She was a religious woman and was among those few women, whose religion had made them beautiful or whose inner beauty had made their religion effective. If Iranzir was a perfect sane husband that any woman could ever wish for, then Fairynelo was an impeccable and sane wife that any man could ever yearn for. Though there had never been any altercation or argument between Iranzir and Fairynelo, yet Iranzir's mother would say, "I think Iranzir and Fairynelo are not happy in their marriage." When somebody would ask her why, she would just reply, "If Fairynelo is a beautiful garden, then she is in the safe hands of a dexterous gardener, Iranzir, who is subconsciously planning to sell off his beautiful garden, which is always subconsciously praying for the death of her dexterous gardener."

We don't know why she would say this. Perhaps she could see what the others could not, or whatever she was saying was a figment of her old mind. Iranzir and Fairynelo would not only care for each other, but also share everything with each other like friends. If Iranzir was late, Fairynelo would wait for him for meals, sometimes till midnight. If Fairynelo did not feel well, Iranzir would attend to the washing and cooking of meals. They were the most coveted couple of Paindise. Whoever saw them together just envied them being in their place.

There was a lot of fuss at Fairynelo's house when Fairynelo and Iranzir reached there. They were welcomed with open arms by Fairynelo's parents.

It was 10:00 p.m. when Fairynelo's friend Qazia Shams learnt of Fairynelo's arrival. She rushed to Fairynelo's home. Fairynelo had just finished combing her hair when she stepped into her room. When Fairynelo saw her, she hugged her friend and ushered her to sit down. They spent happy hours reminiscing about their school days. When Qazia Shams was about to leave, they heard a voice rave, "She turned; I saw her turning...she turned; I saw her turning."

"Who is raving?" enquired Fairynelo.

"It is Musmad. Ever since your departure, he has been raving, 'she turned; I saw her turning.' Your and Musmad's love story is notorious and a slogan at every mouth in Heavel," replied Qazia Shams and left as though she had come to pay some debt.

Fairynelo could not sleep that night as she kept worrying all through the night as to what would happen if Iranzir were to come to know about the foolish love Musmad harboured for her. What would Iranzir think if he came to know Musmad had been incarcerated by the police for harassing her? "I had better leave Heavel early in the morning, and never come here again," mumbled Fairynelo. Despite the insistence of her parents, Fairynelo and Iranzir left early in the morning on the pretext of having some urgent work to do.

Though Iranzir told Fairynelo that they should spend some days with her parents, Fairynelo did not listen to him.

Musmad was sitting at the bend of the road when Iranzir drove by. Musmad caught a passing glimpse of Fairynelo and raved while running behind the car of his dreams, "She turned; I saw her turning... She turned; I saw her turning."

Though Iranzir tried a lot to stop the car to find out why a poor madman was running behind their car, Fairynelo did not let him stop.

Words of Musmad, "She turned; I saw her turning" were reverberating in the ears of Fairynelo and Iranzir long after they had reached home. Iranzir could not comprehend the meaning of those silly words; Fairynelo did not want to comprehend the meaning of those foolish words.

6

The Prophet of Doom

Musmad was invariably busy in finding extraordinary facts about ordinary things. Musmad knew no haste. He would sit, looking at a creeping insect for hours as though there was some hidden secret behind it's creeping, which Musmad was trying to uncover. Watching everything for hours was not Musmad's habit, but a way of living, which spurred him to dig deeper and deeper till he reached the apogee of comprehension where describing him as human was not felicitous, and counting him among angels was not apt, as angels do not say, 'She turned, I saw her turning.' Musmad was not like a child, who runs after colourful butterflies, nor was he like an adult, who despises wasting time in non-lucrative playing with butterflies. He was a perspicacious witness, who witnessed the vulnerable eggs of butterflies, changing their course slowly and dexterously into delicate caterpillars by pure love and care of nature, which eventually led to metamorphosis of ugly chrysalises drenched in nauseating sap into beautiful butterflies. Musmad witnessed the emergence of beautiful butterflies from ugly chrysalis in the lap of nature. It was Musmad, who raved of true beauty in Heavel, "Love and care ugliness until it metamorphoses into beauty, like nature loves and cares the ugly chrysalis until it is transformed into a beautiful butterfly. If you detest ugliness, it will never ripen into beauty, and if it never ripens into beauty, life will lose its meaning and despair will overpower you." Musmad would rave with a lisp.

Musmad was not a man of one place. He was a drifter who spent an itinerant life. After departure of Fairynelo, he started roaming the countryside of Paindise, which was once described as paradise on earth, but was now a battlefield where only innocents were being massacred. Musmad not only roamed on this battlefield, but also rummaged through the ruins of it till he comprehended the nation, which kills its own messengers, destining itself to the doom of war. Paindise was a living epitome of such a nation. It not only killed its own messengers, but also kept them deprived of the shroud. Musmad would usually rave at rallies of politicians, "Neither Polingual nor Marionet, but only Paindise is responsible for its doom."

It was not Musmad, but his eloquence in voicing stinging facts on face, which coerced people into remarking, "Musmad is a prophet of doom."

Musmad was not capricious by nature, nor was he easily predictable. He was a vendor, who sold dreams of knowledge, free and of his own volition. He would talk to people when he wanted; at times he would stop while talking to them without any obvious cause and remain reticent for hours. Usually hours would change into days and days into months. Musmad was a paradox beyond comprehension of people, who construed themselves gods of knowledge. Musmad would be called a saint when seen in prostration, but devil of devils when seen puffing on hallucinogen-filled cigarettes, which was his only means to unveil his Fairynelo. Virtually Musmad would talk to everything, the green trees, which gave him shade in the scorching heat of June, and taught him the real joy of sacrifice; the creeping earthworms, which taught him to cool off the unbearably high temperature of abhorrence by spurting out the cool spring of love from his being. Musmad never got tired of talking to them, as they were the only ones to understand his language of incoherence. They were Musmad's true companions, both in his triumphs and failures, and it seemed as though they were saying, "Yes Musmad, she turned; you saw her turning."

People usually grope for divine and supernatural interventions in the deathly darkness of despair like a child who grabs the hem of his mother's dress in the scary darkness. When caught in the abyss of despair and helplessness, people would run to Musmad for help, misconstruing him as an angel of fate. Musmad would laugh at them and rave, "I could not make turning of my Fairynelo into her returning to me, then tell me, how can I remedy your problems, my friends?"

People still badgered Musmad with their endless complaints.

Elderly people would complain, "Ours sons are not meek and submissive; they don't comply with our wishes. After their marriage, they have changed completely. They are more of their wives. Please do something, as they are the only support in our old age." Musmad would rave while pointing towards the male frogs in a pond, carrying lumps of eggs on their thighs, poised to release young tadpoles, "They are not carrying this burden to produce a group of tadpoles, which will support and bring food for them in their old age, but to produce a new generation, which will value and respect liberty rather than power. Though these frogs will never meet their baby tadpoles in their coming life, still they are carrying them. Learn to think beyond the boundaries of selfishness from these frogs."

No one could comprehend Musmad's raving and his strange examples. The youth would laugh when Musmad raved at them, "Love and respect your parents as worker bees do. They love and nourish the young bees of their queen though they mean nothing to them. Can you not love your old parents, who are your own blood?" But neither the youth nor the elderly people were moved by his eloquence, and found his analogies incomprehensible. Musmad loved everything; it seemed as though there was a cool spring of love emerging from the auricles of his heart, which first flowed through his veins, and after filling his being, spurted out in the form of poignant words, "She turned; I saw her turning."

7

Love Rituals

Night had fallen when Iranzir heard the poignant words of Musmad, "She turned; I saw her turning," while driving home through the dense forest, whose eerie sounds could scare even the loin-hearted man. Not only in Iranzir but also in everyone, the uncanny desire to ask Musmad, "Who turned and you saw her turning?" was born on hearing his plaintive note. It was fraught with danger to stop the car in such a dense and perilous forest at night, yet Iranzir jeopardised his life to see who was repeating those touching words, which moved everyone to tears. The heart-rending words of Musmad were not new for Iranzir for they had been reverberating in his ears ever since his return from Heavel. He got out of the car and eavesdropped on the tear-jerking words to reckon which direction they were coming from. But the cold breeze distracted him each time he was on the verge of fruition. In the light of the moon, Iranzir could just make out shapes and outlines. On failing to figure out the direction from which the heartbreaking words came in the darkness of night, Iranzir climbed onto an embankment, overlooking a beck, and lit a cigarette. By the time he finished his cigarette, the breeze had subsided but the moving ravings were no more audible. Iranzir stubbed out the cigarette and returned to his car. While entering the car, he heard the same words, which would tug at the heartstrings of every beating heart, coming from the beck. He ran to the beck, and saw Musmad sitting at the bottom of the stairs, with legs hanging in the water and repeating, "She turned; I saw her turning...She turned; I saw her turning."

Iranzir sat quietly on the upper step behind Musmad and closed his eyes to meditate on the stirring words, which soon took him deep inside an ocean, where a gigantic lush green ground had been festooned with Christmas lights and sprigs of holly. In this gigantic ground, princes were ensconced on mahogany thrones, facing their beautiful princesses, who too were ensconced on thrones but on the opposite side of the gigantic ground. Behind every prince stood royal male advisors, dressed in black, and who would stoop down every now and then to advise their princes. Princesses too were served by royal female advisors, dressed in white, and they too would bend down to whisper in the ears of their respective princesses. Iranzir witnessed the perplexing spectacle from the centre of the gigantic ground, looking alternately at princes and princesses, who began performing a series of singular and complex love rituals, which were beyond his comprehension. Confounded and baffled, Iranzir opened his eyes as a cold breeze nudged him. 'What a bizarre dream!' murmured Iranzir. The singularity of the dream and his inquisitiveness coerced him into closing his eyes again to unveil the whole spectacle all over again. Soon he entered the same deep ocean, where complex love rituals were being performed in succession.

As soon as the royal female advisors whispered in the ears of the princesses, they stood up and pretended to hug their princes by clasping the air in their arms as though actresses were rehearsing for a waltz. Iranzir chuckled and muttered, "I have never seen such airy hugs." When the princesses got back on the thrones, the princes stood up on the advice of their royal advisors and started sending flying kisses to their respective princesses, who jostled for the flying kisses of their lovers as though hungry herrings were jostling for food. "I wonder whether these flying kisses slake their thirst for love!" mumbled Iranzir in surprise. After completing the second ritual of love, as the royal advisors beckoned, the royal couples sprawled out on their thrones, breathing and panting heavily, as though dog-tired, vanquished kings were sprawled out on the dusty ground after fighting the long battles to recover their lost queens and kingdoms. "Can the pretence of ecstasy really bring joy?" murmured Iranzir frowningly. Suddenly the royal couples got up from the sprawled position as the royal advisors patted them on their shoulders, and began shouting and wailing, but alas, all the shouting was lost and the wails died away before they could cross the immeasurable distance of the gigantic ground. The royal female advisors made their respective princesses sit down cross-legged with handkerchiefs in their right hands and gestured them to wipe away the phony tears trickling down from their respective lovers' eyes, who were pretending to shed tears on the advice of their advisors. The royal couples kept on performing the perplexing series of love rituals on the advice of their advisors. "Who are these foolish royal couples, trying to slake their thirst for love by performing love rituals?" mumbled Iranzir in sleep, while Musmad lay already fast sleep.

Iranzir slept, while Musmad woke up early in the morning and splashed his face with the cold water of the beck. Musmad was in prostration when Iranzir woke up. He rubbed his drowsy eyes and went to the beck to have ablutions. After having ablutions, Iranzir too went into prostration beside Musmad. "Oh my Allah, confer courage on me, so that I can claw my way through the bushy forest of life," prayed Iranzir. "Love rituals...love rituals...foolish royal couples, who were trying to slake their thirst for love by performing love rituals, are those married couples, who do you come cross daily. The royal couples, who seemed to be happy, are two repugnant souls, in truth. The royal couples, who were pretending to be contended with love rituals, are like thirsty men, who try to slake their thirst with empty glasses, thinking them to be filled with water. But for how long... but for how long... but for how long? You too are a royal couple; yes...yes, you are a royal couple," raved Musmad.

As Iranzir heard Musmad's words, he sat up from his prostration and found Musmad talking to himself, with eyes closed. 'Was he referring to me as a royal couple? And how did he come to know about my dream? I think he has mystical powers!' thought Iranzir. Iranzir had begun to comprehend Musmad's bizarre words, but his thoughts were still swimming upstream in the river of vagueness. He again prostrated beside Musmad, who was raving, "Love rituals...love rituals....love rituals...the royal advisors, who would stoop down to advise the royal couples in their ears, are the love books, which couples read daily after waking up and prior to sleeping. Couples learn the rituals of love by heart from these love books, which are written by great writers, who yearn to write great ritualistic love stories, which bring ephemeral happiness, but cannot doll up the bride of life. You too have learnt the love rituals by heart."

Gradually Iranzir realised that the royal couple meant Fairynelo and him while the royal advisors were those thousands of love books, which adorned the mahogany shelves of his house. Tears began to trickle down from

Iranzir's eyes when Musmad uttered his last words, "Love rituals...love rituals...love rituals... the immeasurable distance between the royal couples, in truth, is the immeasurable distance between understanding and perception of married couples, despite sharing the same bed of ecstasy. Wipe away your trickling tears, break the shackles of love rituals and delve deep inside the ocean of your being to explore the coruscating pearl of your love. Write your own love story, devoid of love rituals, with the pen of your soul and the ink of your heart." When Musmad stopped raving, Iranzir had comprehended everything comprehensively.

After remaining prostrated for an hour, Musmad stood up and sat cross-legged under the shade of a *chinar* tree, leaning back against its hefty trunk with eyes closed. Iranzir too sat cross-legged beside Musmad, leaning back but with eyes wide open, staring into space as though trying desperately to weave the trawl net of answers around the wriggling questions pertaining to his dream. "I saw you in Heavel five years ago, running behind my car while raving, 'She turned; I saw her turning.' Why were you chasing my car, and who turned?... Who did you see turning?" asked Iranzir while turning his head slowly towards Musmad, who was fiddling with dry autumn leaves of *chinar* with his right hand.

Musmad remained completely reticent, and even did not open his eyes as though he had not heard Iranzir, as though the voice of Iranzir could not vibrate his eardrums. For a long time, Iranzir waited for a reply from Musmad, who was engrossed in listening to the soft rustle of the big *chinar* leaves, which were dropping down from the branches, one after another, at the slightest nudge of the breeze, after singing the melancholic song of autumn.

When Musmad did not reply, Iranzir lifted his eyes and gazed admiringly at the falling leaves, which were looking frail and exhausted. Perhaps they had travelled a long wearing journey from spring to autumn just like Iranzir, who had experienced an arduous journey from happiness to despair. At last Iranzir too closed his eyes and went back to his old days on the wings of memories. He opened his eyes at dusk and found his head leaning on the left shoulder of Musmad, who was patting him on the head as a mother pats her wriggling baby in her lap. The joy, which Iranzir found by leaning on the shoulder of Musmad, was worth more than all pearls and kingdoms.

When twilight grew darker, Iranzir stood up, and squatted on the ground before Musmad and said, "If you were not to take offence, could I ask how you came to know about my dream of royal couples?"

Silence.... deathly silence! On seeing Musmad unwilling to reply, Iranzir continued, "I had an elder brother, who was a schoolteacher and a very nice human being. He fell in love with a naive looking girl, who used to receive private tuition from him in history. Despite opposition from the society and their families, they got married. For five years, they led a happy, married life, each sacrificing his or her joy for the sake of the other. If one had a headache, the other would press his forehead all through the night. They not only sacrificed their sleep, but also renounced their families and the society for each other. Their love made the whole society feel guilty at ostracising such an adorable and cute couple. One day, quite unexpectedly, they decided to get divorced. Their decision to seek divorce was a bolt from the blue for me and all who knew about their love. I never talked to my brother ever since their divorce as I considered him the main culprit in the divorce. Whenever he was asked, 'Why did you get divorced?' his stock reply was, 'You cannot comprehend and I cannot explain, as I myself do not know the reason for divorce.' I always abhorred him for divorcing his wife though his wife too wanted it. I did not even attend his funeral when he died as I felt he should have tried to reconcile their differences mutually. However, now I have comprehended his predicament, as I am myself in the same quandary. Now I have comprehended; we do not love but just perform the rituals of love, which have already been laid down for us by great writers and which every generation has been inheriting as a legacy from its ancestors. Performing the same love rituals over generations has deceived us into believing that the love rituals are souvenirs of love. But for how long can couples slake their thirst for pure love and affection by love rituals. They eventually get fed up with the love rituals, and find themselves in a predicament, where it is impossible for them to answer their own questions. They slowly start hating each other and soon the hate changes to abhorrence and the same couples, who were construed as the epitome of love, start subconsciously praying for the death of each other. It is virtually impossible for poor couples to comprehend the reason for abhorrence for their spouse as they have misconstrued the love rituals as true love. When unable to comprehend the reason for the subconscious abhorrence for their spouse, couples choose to take divorce. There are crores of couples, who are sacrificed on the altar of love rituals, as they are hard to comprehend and impossible to explain. I am lucky, as I have understood my problem by the virtue of my dream of the royal couples. Till yesterday, I could not reply to questions of my friends when they asked why I wanted divorce despite having no altercation or problem with my wife. I would remain silent, as I knew they could not comprehend and I could not explain the reason for my divorce. Though I am getting divorced in seven days, I am contended, as I know now the reason for wanting divorce. Now I know that neither my wife nor I, but only the love rituals, are responsible for our divorce. I am so hapless that I cannot make my wife understand the reason for our divorce. Even if I were to try to make her understand, she would not listen to me as the love rituals are imprinted on her mind and heart, and it is virtually impossible to erase them from her heart and mind with the rubber of reason. I know nothing is going to change. People will fall in love during their teens and get tied in the relationship of marriage, which would ultimately culminate in divorce or compromise as the boat of love rituals is destined to sink. I am so fed up with my married life that I do not want to go home for these seven days. What would you do if you were I? Tell me...please tell."

Iranzir tried a lot to persuade Musmad into replying to his questions, but failed. It grew completely dark. Iranzir and Musmad could only make out the silhouettes of each other in the light of the moon. Late at night, Musmad took some food and two filthy plates from his grimy tattered bag, and without saying anything, he offered to Iranzir a wonderful supper, which he had never eaten before. Musmad himself ate quickly and lay down on his back to doze off to sleep. Iranzir tried a lot to eat something, but could not and eventually leaned back against the *chinar* trunk. He gazed into space for hours as though trying to console himself, and ultimately he too fell into deep sleep.

People start performing love rituals as soon as they fall in love. Their first ritual of love is lurking for hours outside the palace of the queen of their heart, making them leave everything behind, their studies, daily appointments and all else. They even know the colour of the paint of their beloved's neighbour's house, but this ritual of love becomes meaningless as soon as their beloved accepts their proposal. The second love ritual of talking on the phone all through the night with their beloved provides evanescent joy to lovers. But alas, lovers soon get fed up with the monotony of talking the same thing every night. As they proceed to touch the zenith of love, which is marriage, love rituals become more and more monotonous. Married couples start their maiden love ritual on the bed of ecstasy. They relentlessly say to each other in a husky voice while playing the game of inheritance, "I love you. I cannot live without you...I love you; I cannot live without you." But alas, the strength and significance of these words gets diluted as the water of time gets mixed with it. Soon the couples find themselves in a quandary, which has only two doors, one leading to compromise and the other, to divorce. Iranzir and Fairynelo had chosen the door of divorce.

Next morning, Iranzir woke up early and saw Musmad in prostration. He did not want to disturb Musmad, who was deeply engrossed in the worship of Allah. So he decided to leave quietly. When he reached the stairs of the beck, he heard Musmad repeating in prostration, "She turned; I saw her turning. Make her turning into her returning to you by breaking the shackles of love rituals. Do not miss a day. Seven days are enough to break the yoke of love rituals.

Pierce the dark veil of love rituals, which hangs on her drowsy eyes, with the arrows of proportionate love. Love... love her in these seven days but love as a father loves his daughter. Disproportionate love is the cause of ailments. Splurge your proportionate love on her, unlike the mother who lavishes disproportionate love on her baby. Neither sacrifices your joys nor let her to sacrifice, so that love will not become a burden on your heart, but a sweet honey, which you always yearn to savour. Love her proportionately, as a father loves his daughter, but unlike the father, clasp your hands, close your eyes and pray to your Allah when she is being sent off with her groom, 'Oh my Allah, make her turning into her returning to me forever.' Do not think about selling off your beautiful garden, but sit on its gazebo to appreciate its beauty and vista of life. Water your beautiful garden proportionately, so that it will not pray for your death because both over-watering and under-watering cause withering and wilting. Go... go, encash your dreams before they get lost in the distance."

Iranzir listened to Musmad's words without turning his head. It was apparent from his relaxed face that he had imbibed Musmad's words comprehensively. He got into his car and drove straight home.

At dusk, Iranzir knocked three times on the door of Fairynelo's room, waiting for her permission. It was the first time, Iranzir had rapped on the door of her room before entering, ever since their marriage. Fairynelo was on her bed, lying back against the pillow. When she saw Iranzir standing at the door, she sat up, titivated her hair and scarf as though she had seen a stranger at the door. Fairynelo dropped her eyes and began to tie and untie the thread, which hung loose at the edge of the bedsheet as Iranzir came in. As he sat down beside Fairynelo, she shrank back against the headboard of the bed. Iranzir had never seen Fairynelo behave like this. For a long time, they remained completely silent and at last Iranzir spoke, "We have enjoyed many ecstasies and climaxes on this four-poster bed, under its yellow canopy, but those ecstasies and climaxes, rather the love rituals were not strong enough to keep us tied in the bond of love. This bed is witness to our endless pillow talks, which would continue all through the night, but alas, the endless pillow talks were not potent enough to prevent the thread of our marriage from breaking. We never lied to each other; we never deceived each other. Then what is the reason for seeking divorce? This question is yet to be answered."

Fairynelo was scratching the bedpost in nervousness while Iranzir was talking to her. After a brief pause, Iranzir continued, "You sacrificed all your joys and ambitions for me. I know, your burning ambition was to study medicine, but you gave up your medical career just to look after me. You never visited your parents just because you thought I would be lonely without you. You kept on sacrificing your joys without grumbling until you got exhausted. I did the same. I too sacrificed my leisure and liberty for you. I never spent time with my friends just because I feared that you would feel forlorn without me. I too kept on sacrificing my happiness at the altar of your joys till I became enervated. Why did we sacrifice our joys for each other? The answer is very simply that we have been taught to sacrifice our joys for each other thinking it to be true love. If sacrificing everything for each other is true love, then why are we on the brink of partition despite sacrificing everything for each other? The reason is simple: sacrificing happiness and joys for each other is nothing but the love ritual, which our ancestors have taught us for generations, and that is the sole reason for our divorce. Ever since our marriage, we only performed the rituals of love. We never loved each other proportionately. I want to give another chance to our marriage. I want to love you rather than performing the love rituals. Fairynelo, fate has given us a chance; let us make the best of it. Let us love rather than performing the rituals."

As a cold breeze seeped in through the window, fluttering the yellow canopy of the bed, Fairynelo said in a husky whisper, "I do not think there is anything left in the ruins of our marriage, which is worthy to be kissed. I think we had better get divorced without delay, irrespective of what the reason for our divorce is."

Fairynelo looked very resolute and determined. When Iranzir realised that it was now impossible to get the derailed train of their marriage back on track, he said, "As you wish, but please do not sacrifice anything for me in these seven days. Let me doll up these seven days. Let me fall in true love, devoid of rituals."

Fairynelo was expecting Iranzir to sleep with her, but he just kissed her on the forehead, tucked her in and said, "Goodnight, my parting love."

After switching off the lights of her room, Iranzir closed the door and went to the guest room, where he squatted down against the wall, weeping profusely at the thought of imminent separation as though feeling the pangs of coming partition.

Next morning, Iranzir woke up early and brewed some coffee for himself and Fairynelo, who preferred coffee early in the morning. He felt a surreal joy and unusual thrill in brewing coffee for Fairynelo; a thrill that he had never felt before. You may wonder if Iranzir's brewing coffee for Fairynelo did not amount to a love ritual! No it does not, simply because Fairynelo did not expect Iranzir to brew coffee for her, and that too early in the morning. Every ritual, whether a love ritual or any other ritual, is anticipated or rather expected, but true love comes always with surprises and smiles. Iranzir entered Fairynelo's room with two cups of coffee, offered one to Fairynelo and said,

"I want you to resume your medical profession, which you had forsaken for me. I want to return your liberty and ambitions, which you had smothered for a smooth running of our marriage. Now get ready within ten minutes, for you are to resume your duty today, Dr. Fairynelo."

When Fairynelo heard Iranzir calling her Dr. Fairynelo, she smiled a small smile. She tried a lot to evade Iranzir, but could not. At last she said, "As I am returning to my parents' home in seven days, I had better resume my medical career there. By the way, guests do not bedeck their dreams where uncertainty is the host."

Iranzir simply rubbed his eyelids and replied, "It is true, guests do not festoon their dreams where uncertainty is the host, but daughters do bedeck their tender dreams in the secure lap of their father's home. You are not my guest, but my lost daughter, who I found last night."

On hearing Iranzir refer to her as 'his lost daughter', Fairynelo burst into tears and wept like a baby. Iranzir patted her on the head and continued, "I will send you off with your groom amidst great fanfare. Despite relentless rain at your marriage, people will applaud and give a standing ovation as you hug him. Please Fairynelo, spend these six-days with me happily. Let me make these six days memorable. Now go and get ready."

As Fairynelo went into the washroom to get ready, Iranzir mumbled to himself, "Yes Fairynelo, people will give a standing ovation as you hug me. I know you love me very much. I know you will never desert me alone in the desolate forest of life."

After dropping Fairynelo off at the hospital, Iranzir left for his private clinic, where he attended to patients from 9:00 a.m. to 10:00 a.m.

Fairynelo felt happy and secure; perhaps she was now in the reliable hands of a loving father.

Four days passed, but Fairynelo did not feel as if she was getting divorced. Though Iranzir never said to her in those four days that he loved her or missed her, yet Fairynelo felt as if she was in deep love with Iranzir. On the fifth day, Fairynelo returned home late at night. But Iranzir merely remarked, "Dr. Fairynelo, you should not work so much. It can deteriorate your health."

Fairynelo replied, "Okay, in future, I will take care to return home on time." Fairynelo had started to learn that loving each other proportionately is certainly better than loving each other blindly as blind love always stumbles over sacrifices and falls in the ditch of the love rituals. Neither Fairynelo nor Iranzir got fed up of each other in those five days.

When the sun arose on the sixth day, Iranzir said to Fairynelo, "You are parting from me tomorrow. If you allow me, I want to buy some clothes of my choice for you."

Without performing any ritual, Fairynelo replied, "Okay, when are we going for shopping?"

"Right away," replied Iranzir, smilingly.

They went downtown to indulge in some serious shopping. Iranzir bought a number of dresses for Fairynelo, but the most special yet foolish items to buy were a white hanky and a silver bracelet. The eve of the seventh day passed very quickly and soon time came for Fairynelo's departure.

It was raining ruthlessly when Fairynelo finished her packing. After getting ready, she came out, holding her bag in the hand and said to Iranzir, who was waiting for her at the outer door, "My grandmother was wrong. One should not believe in 'love at first sight' as it breaks one's heart."

Iranzir looked into her wet eyes and replied, "I do not know why, but today I want to get drenched to the skin in this relentless rain. In this persistent rain I have to tell you a lot, as I do not want you to see my falling tears because I look very childish while crying. Will you come with me in this unrelenting rain for the last time?"

Fairynelo smiled and nodded her head. They went into the inexorable rain, hand in hand. But on reaching the centre of the yard, they stopped and Iranzir said, while leaving her hand, "My grandfather too was wrong. One should not marry the girl, who believes in 'love at first sight' as it is nothing but a silly love ritual. But I had married the perfectly right girl."

As Fairynelo left for her home, Iranzir knelt down, closed his eyes, clasped his hands and said, "Oh my Allah, confer the beautiful garden back on the dexterous gardener as he has understood that he is valueless without his garden."

Alas, ego played its role. Fairynelo did not turn despite wanting to do so. Iranzir too wanted to stop her, but ego prevented him from letting his train of dreams go.

Later Iranzir spent many years in reminiscing about those memorable seven days. He would always talk about those seven days and if someone asked, "Why do you talk only about those seven days?" he would reply, "I did not spend those seven days; that was Musmad who did so. I merely played his role just as an actor plays the role of a character in a play."

Five years later, Iranzir entered into a second marriage with a fellow doctor, but lived a life of compromise thereafter. He never tried to teach his wife the difference between love and love rituals. Perhaps he knew that what had been inculcated in our minds for many millenniums could not be removed in one go. Fairynelo too got married to her cousin and led a life of compromise thereafter. But now and then she would sit on the windowsill of her room and go back to those distant seven days, the seven days of pure love, the seven days of her true happiness. She too loved to talk of those seven days of love. When someone would ask her, "Why do you always reminisce about those seven days?" she would inevitably reply, "If I ever loved somebody, it was Iranzir of those seven days."

8

The King of Goodbye

After twenty years, Musmad found everything in Heavel as it was, except that the people who had been young and used to ridicule Musmad had grown old. People who had been old and used to laugh at Musmad had passed away and were atoning for their sins in the serenity of their graves. Children who used to mock at Musmad's helplessness had blossomed into youth, and golden daughters and ruthless kings, who were stretching their limbs in the secure wombs of their mothers, had opened their eyes in this world of struggle, strife and challenge. Musmad looked older than his age. He was only fifty-years old, but he looked sixty or sixty-five. Musmad was a year younger than Fairynelo, yet there were more wrinkles on his face than there were on Fairynelo's. Musmad's upright posture had now stooped low and he walked as though carrying a heavy load on his back.

On returning to Heavel, Musmad roamed aimlessly around the streets and eventually stopped at the *chinar* tree, where he had wept copiously when Fairynelo was being engaged to Iranzir. He touched the soft leaves with his quivering hands while mumbling to himself, "You have still preserved her smell. Thank you my companions, for keeping the fragrance of her body intact."

Musmad had long been forgotten by the people of Heavel, but the trees, which used to listen to his plight without yawning, and the wind, which was his lover's go-between, never forgot him. His feeble body, which could hardly stand for long, his quaking hands, which could barely hold a glass of water and his twitching lips, which could scarcely utter a word coherently, belied his inner youthfulness, which always cajoled him into raving, "She turned; I saw her turning." The people of Heavel did not recognise Musmad; perhaps he was not worthy to be remembered or probably their minds were not worthy enough to remember him.

Fairynelo's second husband, Attiffal, was a chemistry professor, who was on the verge of retirement. He did not have any hobbies besides taking his black cow with white spots along the riverbank for grazing after college hours. Whosoever of his age he met while taking his cow for grazing, he would ask, "Are you satisfied with your life?"

If someone replied 'no', he would shake his hand warmly, but if someone replied 'yes', he would give a scornful laugh and say, "I know you are lying. But, my friend, who are you lying to? Me or yourself."

Attiffal was the most candid person in Heavel for he could say anything on one's face honestly. Mostly he used to speak to his black cow and scold it if it gobbled up the grass, and said, "You should not devour the grass like this. It does not compliment my cow."

One day he saw Musmad sitting at the bottom of the stairs, which led to the river, when he was grazing his cow on the fresh green grass of riverside. He went over to Musmad and sat by him. He rubbed his forehead with his right hand for some time, as though he had recognised Musmad, but could not recall his name despite trying hard to recall. At last he nudged Musmad and exclaimed, "Oh Musmad, where have you been for such a long time?"

But Musmad did not react. When Attiffal saw his cow wandering away, he ran to shepherd it towards the riverside.

After shepherding the cow, he came back to Musmad and said, "All people start their life with a dream in their eyes to become world famous, but end up with a twinge of regret in their hearts and pang of remorse in their minds. Doctors remorse for being doctors; actors mourn for being actors when they are on the verge of death. In my life I have never come across even a single person contended with his life. At the end of life, everybody wails and laments for spending their life as they have spent. I do not know why, but I feel you are contended with your life. Perhaps you did not start your life with the dream of becoming famous."

When Attiffal was talking to Musmad, his black cow wandered off. He rushed to shepherd it and advised the cow in a husky whisper, "When I am talking to somebody, do not pester me, as I do not like this." This time Attiffal tethered the cow to a stake so it would not wander away.

After tethering the cow, he came back to Musmad and continued, "You are the king of goodbye, who kissed all his sorrows and happinesses goodbye. You are the king of loss, who lost everything to fate except for the few words of consolation, 'She turned; I saw her turning.' You kept on losing your possessions without complaining. You completed your journey from the cradle to the grave without regrets. When I was young, I used to hurl stones at you, thinking you did not feel pain. I love you Musmad, I love you for being the king of goodbye." Attiffal cuddled Musmad close and wept.

Musmad lit a hallucinogen-filled cigarette and puffed on it until it grew dark. Attiffal deliberately did not talk about Fairynelo. Perhaps his ego did not let him speak despite being so outspoken. Attiffal knew Fairynelo and Musmad's love story, as he knew them since childhood.

Late at night, when Attiffal and Fairynelo were in bed, he said to Fairynelo, "Do you know, I saw the mad Musmad, who used to badger you when you were a schoolgirl. He still says, 'She turned; I saw her turning'."

Attiffal's words sounded more friendly and less taunting, so Fairynelo did not take his words seriously. By now her blonde tresses had turned grey, the soft skin of her face had developed scars of old age and she had long ago bid farewell to her youth, which was the only reason for her conceit. Fairynelo was now not only an old woman, but also a mother of three daughters.

Next day, at noon, Fairynelo was in her room when someone rang the doorbell. She went to answer the door and saw Attiffal standing at the doorstep. "Goodness gracious! What are you doing here at this time? Have you skived off the college again today? I do not know, what is going to happen to your poor chemistry students. I wish Allah saved them," Fairynelo taunted Attiffal.

Attiffal retorted, "Ha, you hoary woman, your mind has gone senile. You always nag an eminent chemistry professor like me and by the way HCl and H_2SO_4 are not going to flee; my genius students can learn them any time. Let them enjoy their youth today. Never mind, you cannot comprehend such things, which are made for intellectuals, as you are completely crazy. I am not desirous of seeing your wrinkled face. I have brought my 'king of goodbye' to have lunch with me. Here is my 'king of loss' and my 'king of goodbye'."

Fairynelo was about to bellow at Attiffal, when she saw the frail Musmad. She clenched her finger between her teeth and exclaimed, "Oh my goodness, he is really back!" Fairynelo shrank against the wall, but tried to deal the situation with equanimity.

Attiffal made Musmad sit on the ground and ordered Fairynelo, "What are you looking at, like an owl? Go and fetch some food for two intellectuals."

Though Fairynelo tried a lot to persuade Attiffal to take lunch in the dinning-room, Attiffal insisted, "We want to savour lunch and not the dinning room."

Fairynelo gazed at Musmad while he was taking small mouthfuls of food with his quaking hands as though a toddler was trying to relish a strawberry with his trembling hands. After having lunch, Musmad licked his fingers while Attiffal went into the washroom.

When Attiffal was in the washroom, Fairynelo squatted down before Musmad to clean the dribble around his mouth and heard him mumbling, "She turned; I saw her turning."

She drew nearer to Musmad until her ample bosoms touched Musmad's chest and her dry lips kissed Musmad's filthy right ear-lobe. She whispered in his ear, "It is your delusion. She did not turn; you did not see her turning."

When Fairynelo was going to the kitchen for washing the dishes, Musmad raved behind, "I swear by Allah, she turned; I saw her turning. These fools did not see her turning."

That night Fairynelo could not sleep as she was engaged in reckoning what she had lost and what she had earned!

Musmad would always sit at the lowermost step of the steps, leading to the river, puffing away on hallucinogen-filled cigarettes that conjured up a vivid picture of twenty-year-old Fairynelo in the air. Seeing Fairynelo was not a need of Musmad, but his life. If it had been a need, he might have long ago substituted it by something else, but it was his life and life is never replaced by anything. It can only be chopped into pieces by the sharp sword of death.

One day Musmad was puffing at a hallucinogen-filled cigarette on the riverbank, when Fairynelo happened to pass by. Seeing no one around, she squatted down before Musmad to find out if he could really recognise her. Musmad took a long puff on cigarette and saw his twenty-year old Fairynelo coming out from the heart of the river, as usual wet and hot at the same time. She came and sat by him, her head leaning on his left shoulder. Musmad closed his eyes and continued puffing on the cigarette. Seeing Musmad engrossed in himself, the aged Fairynelo mumbled, "He has forgotten me long before."

Fairynelo was again wrong in her judgement. Musmad had not forgotten her, but had stopped time at youth by perpetually puffing away on hallucinogen-filled cigarettes. He had prevented Fairynelo from physical dilapidation by keeping her in the evergreen forest of his thoughts and deciduous forest of hallucinogenic smoke. Whenever lost in reverie, he would see a nineteen-year old Musmad waltzing twenty-year-old Fairynelo across the lush green floor in relentless rain. Musmad had preserved his youthfulness and Fairynelo's beauty at the cost of his own health.

Musmad was no addict of hallucinogen. He puffed away on the hallucinogenic cigarettes to catch the ephemeral glimpse of Fairynelo. Puffing at cigarettes had brought him to the brink of death.

Fairynelo was on her way home in a bus when she saw her former husband Iranzir sitting behind her. She turned back and smiled at him, but did not exchange courtesies with him. "Thanks for those seven days. The seven days of my triumph. The seven days of my true love, devoid of rituals," confessed Fairynelo, while turning her head back to the front.

"That was not I; that was Musmad, who conferred those seven days of true love on you. I was a mere actor, playing his role," replied Iranzir.

On hearing Iranzir's words, Fairynelo beckoned to the bus conductor to stop the bus and got off. She took a desolate route and walked slowly. A cold breeze blew her locks of grey hair, which were no longer attractive. When she reached the riverbank, she plonked herself down to contemplate on her life. Fairynelo thought, it did not befit her to fall in love now. "What would happen if my daughters came to know about me and Musmad? And I should not think about Musmad, as it is futile now," muttered Fairynelo to herself.,

She embarked on a boat, which sailed smoothly across the river. On disembarking, she saw Musmad sitting on the riverbank. She sat down beside him and said, "If you were not mad, and if I had known that you were my love, I would have married you. Now I am old. I do not have enough courage to transgress the mores laid down by society."

Musmad remained completely reticent. After a few days, Musmad unexpectedly left Heavel, the garden of his dreams.

9

The Cremation

Everybody was relishing sleep when the gory spectacle of Musmad's death was being enacted at the railway station of Heartfeeler, the capital of Polingual, thousands of kilometres away from Heavel. Shortly after midnight, Musmad burped out chunks of congealed blood while coughing. He slowly crawled to an iron pillar, which supported the railway-station roof and leaned against its hard iron bars. He could not help coughing. Each time he coughed, clots of blood belched out through his mouth. Musmad felt as though his lungs were being hauled out. He folded his arms tightly over his chest and pressed them in, to alleviate the cutting pain. Looking cadaverous, perhaps he was at the threshold of death. He closed his eyes and sat peacefully for some time as though he was rummaging through the ruins of his past for the last time.

At dawn, Musmad opened his eyes, and lit a hallucinogen-filled cigarette to see his Fairynelo for the last time on the billowing smoke. He took three long puffs on the cigarette and as he turned his head to the right, he saw Master

Shamag dressed in green, sitting beside him. Musmad smiled faintly at him and said, "Have you come from heaven to take me away with you, my master?"

Shamag nodded yes and Musmad slowly leaned his head on the master's shoulder and said, "See, my master, what has happened to your Musmad. Your Musmad cannot breathe as it pains him. He cannot weep as it heightens his ache. He feels as though his chest is being gnawed away by sharp teeth. Your vanquished king could neither get his kingdom nor his queen back, my master. Your king has lost the battle."

Musmad had never recounted his woes to anybody except Shamag, as he alone could comprehend him. He again took three long puffs on the cigarette and continued, "Your Musmad tried a lot to make people understand that he has a heart which beats like theirs but they always said, 'Musmad, how can you fall in love as you are not one of us, as you are covered with filth, as you do not feel pain, as you walk barefoot on the snow? My master, your Musmad endeavoured a lot to remove the curtain of ignorance and ego from their eyes, but failed desperately. Neither the people of Heavel nor my Fairynelo could peer through my filth. No one stood with me in my triumphs and failures, besides you and my natural companions. Take your Musmad in your arms, my master, as he does not want to stay here any longer."

Musmad wept and bent forward until he went into prostration. After some time, he sat up and puffed again three long puffs on the cigarette and said while closing his eyes, "Let us go from here, my master, as I do not want to stay here. Let us go from here, my master."

Master Shamag tapped Musmad on the right shoulder and said, "My son, open your eyes and see, the whole of Heavel has come to celebrate your long-awaited union with Fairynelo."

But Musmad did not open his eyes and just replied, "They must have come to hurl stones at me, my master."

Master Shamag tapped him again three to four times on the shoulder and said, "No fool, see Iranzir too has come with Fairynelo. They all have come to apologise to you for their mistakes."

Musmad quickly opened his eyes but the mist of death had blurred his vision. He desperately rubbed his eyes and said, "I cannot see anything, my master. Tell me what is happening?"

Shamag cuddled him close and said, "There are people around, yet Fairynelo has taken off her clothes as Iranzir gestured to her at you. The sky could not endure her body in nude for long, so it eventually succumbed to temptation and started a relentless rain." When Master Shamag was depicting the spectacle of confluence of Fairynelo and Musmad, he again belched out lumps of congealed blood. Shamag held him close to his chest and continued, "See, my son, it has started a relentless rain... rain that touched her hair... rain that kissed her cheeks... rain that drenched her lips... rain that trickled down the nape of her neck... rain that made its way through the channel between her burgeoning bosoms... rain that has now become priceless... rain that is now pious..." As Musmad coughed and spewed up blood again. Shamag continued quickly, "Fairynelo has run to Musmad...Fairynelo has run to Musmad."

Musmad besought to Shamag while thrashing his chest with his feeble hands and said in a coarse voice, which slowly dropped to a whisper, "Stop her, my master, please stop her as I know she will say, 'You are a fool who misconstrued my sympathy as love'."

Shamag calmed Musmad's nerves by patting his back and said, "No, my son, see she has only come for you. See, her white, wet *dupatta* has slipped down and now she is stark naked."

Shamag tried to cajole Musmad into opening his eyes, by saying, "See, my son, everybody can see the breathtaking spectacle except Musmad, who lies sprawled on the muddy ground with blood and bruises all over his face as though he is having a sleep after fighting a long battle of his love. See, my son, Fairynelo has crouched over Musmad and priceless drops of rain have lost their grip over her, and fall over Musmad's eyes."

Musmad thrashed his hands at Shamag as though imploring him to tell him fast as he had little time. Shamag speeded up his words and continued, "...Priceless drops of rain lost their grip over Fairynelo and fell over Musmad's eyes... Eyes that knew, she would come... eyes that longed for her... eyes that have been made to see her... see, my son."

Shamag accelerated his words for the last punch and exclaimed, "See, my son, Musmad has stood up with difficulty and Fairynelo hugged him... Eyes into eyes... people around started clapping and gave a standing ovation as Fairynelo kissed Musmad on the forehead... listen son... listen..."

Master Shamag made Musmad stand up, and both were poised to leave for heaven as though he had come to make Musmad live his dream. While leaving the railway station, Shamag called out loudly, "Fairynelo said to Musmad, 'Do you know why I am in nude?' But Musmad shook his head. 'My vanquished king, you have got your kingdom and queen back as Fairynelo is confessing and saying, 'I am punishing my body; I am humiliating it for keeping you deprived of my love. I am sorry, my love, as I could not peer through your filth, as I could not see the sea of love that is lying below your filth.' You were true, my love, I turned; you saw me turning."

When day broke, Musmad was lying dead on the platform with a burning stub of cigarette between his fingers and bloodstains all over the floor. After three days, Musmad was cremated in Heartfeeler by some virtuous Hindus, who did not know him.

GOLDEN CLASSICS

COMPLETE & UNABRIDGED

Charles and Mary Lamb

- Tales from Shakespeare .... 320 pp; Rs. 80

George Orwell

- 1984 .... 320 pp; Rs. 195
- Animal Farm .... 128 pp; Rs. 95

Kahlil Gibran

- The Prophet .... 128 pp; Rs. 60
- The Broken Wings .... 120 pp; Rs. 60
- A Tear and a Smile .... 176 pp; Rs. 60
- Selected Works of Gibran .... 320 pp; Rs. 145

Lewis Carroll

- Alice in Wonderland .... 128 pp; Rs. 60

Rabindranath Tagore

- Gitanjali .... 128 pp; Rs. 60

Robert Louis Stevenson

- Treasure Island .... 224 pp; Rs. 70

Rudyard Kipling

- The Jungle Book .... 192 pp; Rs. 70
- Tales from India .... 320 pp; Rs. 125
- Kim .... 312 pp; Rs. 125

William Shakespeare

- Romeo and Juliet .... 128 pp; Rs. 60
- Macbeth .... 128 pp; Rs. 60